Disney

CLUB PENGUIN™

STUCK ON PUFFLES

Grosset & Du~~nlap~~

978-0-448-45054-4   10 9 8 7 6 5 4 3 2 1

THE PET SHOP

Welcome to the Pet Shop, where penguins can buy their very own puffles! These furry pets make great companions as long as you take good care of them.

What Is a Puffle?

Puffles are cute, fluffy creatures that make perfect pets! They come in seven colors: blue, pink, green, black, purple, red, and yellow.

Adopting Your Puffle

So you're ready to adopt? Click on the Adopt a Puffle catalog in the Pet Shop. Hopefully you've been saving up, because each puffle costs eight hundred coins! Once you adopt a puffle, you can find it in your igloo.

Penguins can adopt as many as fourteen puffles if they have a membership. Penguins without memberships can adopt up to two puffles.

TAKING CARE OF YOUR PUFFLE

To keep your puffle happy and healthy, you need to give it food, exercise, and rest.

Time to Eat

You can feed your puffle Puffle-Os, cookies, and bubble gum. Puffle-Os are the best food for your puffle.

Cookies and bubble gum are tasty but they are not very nutritious. Too many will bring its health bar down. If your puffle is happy and you feed it a treat, it will do a trick. If it is unhappy and you feed it a treat, it will stick its tongue out!

Get Your Move On

Puffles like walks. Click the leash on your puffle's player card and it will follow you. Just make sure your puffle is rested and has been well fed. When you're finished, open up your player card and click on your puffle. It will return to your igloo.

You can play with your puffle by clicking the ball icon on your puffle's player card. Just be sure your puffle has had enough food and rest before you play!

MORE TAKING CARE
OF YOUR PUFFLE

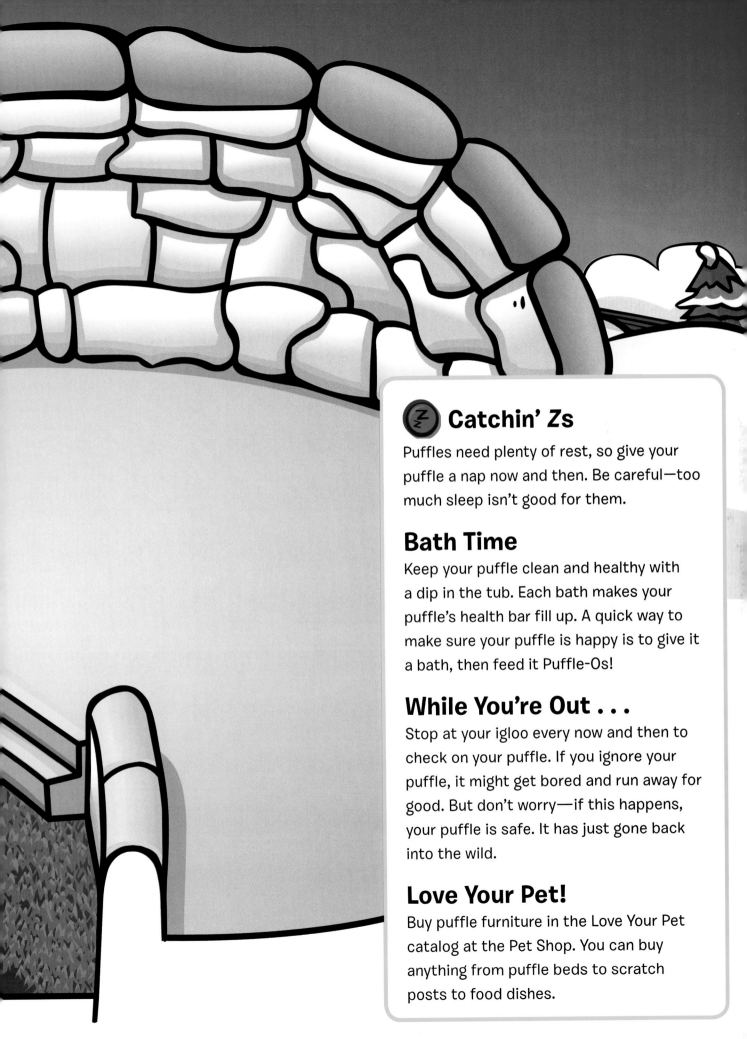

💤 Catchin' Zs

Puffles need plenty of rest, so give your puffle a nap now and then. Be careful—too much sleep isn't good for them.

Bath Time

Keep your puffle clean and healthy with a dip in the tub. Each bath makes your puffle's health bar fill up. A quick way to make sure your puffle is happy is to give it a bath, then feed it Puffle-Os!

While You're Out . . .

Stop at your igloo every now and then to check on your puffle. If you ignore your puffle, it might get bored and run away for good. But don't worry—if this happens, your puffle is safe. It has just gone back into the wild.

Love Your Pet!

Buy puffle furniture in the Love Your Pet catalog at the Pet Shop. You can buy anything from puffle beds to scratch posts to food dishes.

BLUE PUFFLE

Blue puffles were the first puffles on Club Penguin! They are great for a first-time puffle owner because they are are easygoing and are happy most of the time. They are also very loyal pets. Plus, both penguins with memberships and penguins without memberships can adopt them!

Playful Puffle

Blue puffles love to bounce around a ball. Click the *play* icon on the blue puffle's player card. The blue puffle will jump up and down on the ball and roll it back and forth across the floor. Click it again and your puffle will bounce the ball on its head and then balance it on its nose.

Hungry, Hungry Puffle

When you give a blue puffle a piece of gum, it will blow a small bubble and suck the bubble inside its mouth. Then it will open its mouth and show the gum to you! When a blue puffle eats a cookie, it runs back and forth across it, munching the cookie with its big teeth.

RED PUFFLE

Rockhopper, the pirate penguin, brought red puffles to Club Penguin on his ship, the *Migrator*. Rockhopper even has his own pet red puffle named Yarr. Red puffles are the only puffles not originally from Club Penguin. Red puffles are enthusiastic, fearless, and always up for adventure! These puffles can be adopted by both penguins with and without memberships.

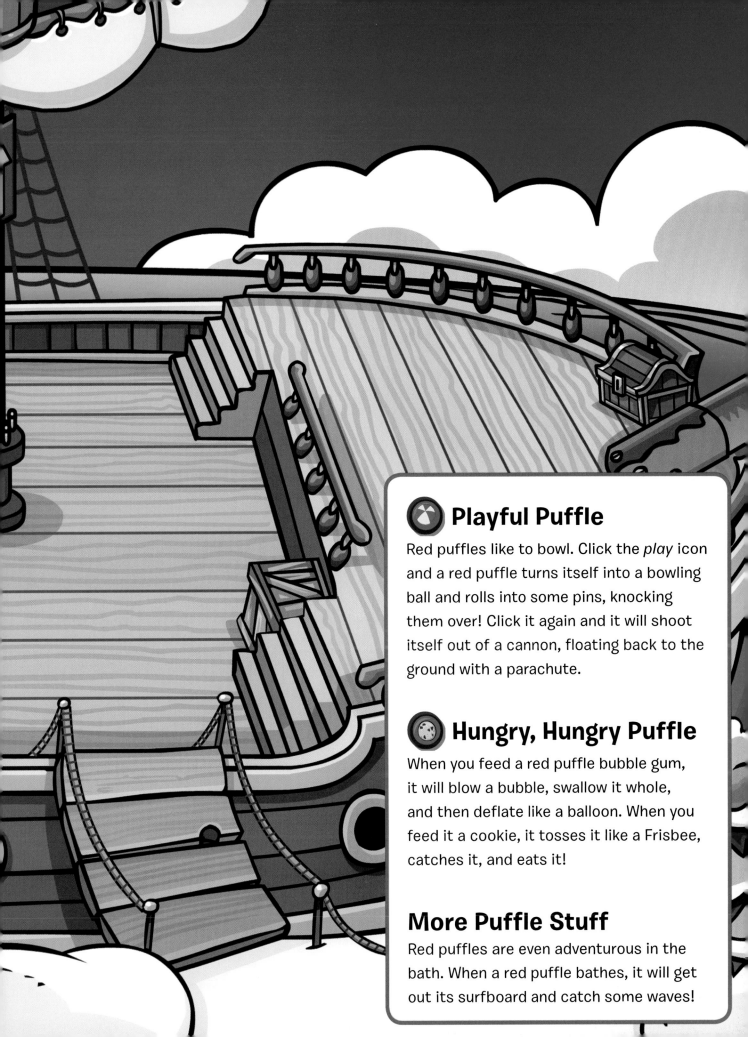

🔴 Playful Puffle

Red puffles like to bowl. Click the *play* icon and a red puffle turns itself into a bowling ball and rolls into some pins, knocking them over! Click it again and it will shoot itself out of a cannon, floating back to the ground with a parachute.

🍪 Hungry, Hungry Puffle

When you feed a red puffle bubble gum, it will blow a bubble, swallow it whole, and then deflate like a balloon. When you feed it a cookie, it tosses it like a Frisbee, catches it, and eats it!

More Puffle Stuff

Red puffles are even adventurous in the bath. When a red puffle bathes, it will get out its surfboard and catch some waves!

GREEN PUFFLE

Green puffles are full of energy and are very playful. They are great at clowning around. There's no question about it: Green puffles are the silliest puffles there are.

🎮 Playful Puffle

A green puffle is very silly at playtime. Click the *play* icon and it will ride its unicycle and juggle until it falls off. Click the *play* icon again and it will do a backward somersault, put on its propeller hat, and fly around the room.

🍪 Hungry, Hungry Puffle

If you feed a green puffle gum, it'll blow a dog-shaped balloon. If you give it a cookie, it will jump on the cookie to break it into little pieces. Then it will act like a vacuum cleaner, sucking the pieces into its mouth.

More Puffle Stuff

After a green puffle gets out of the bath, it uses a hair dryer to dry off. When you dance with a green puffle, it hovers in the air with its propeller hat. In its sleep, it snoozes with its tongue hanging out.

PINK PUFFLE

Pink puffles were first spotted hanging out at the Snow Forts. They are very cheerful, pleasant puffles. They have a lot of energy, and they love to exercise.

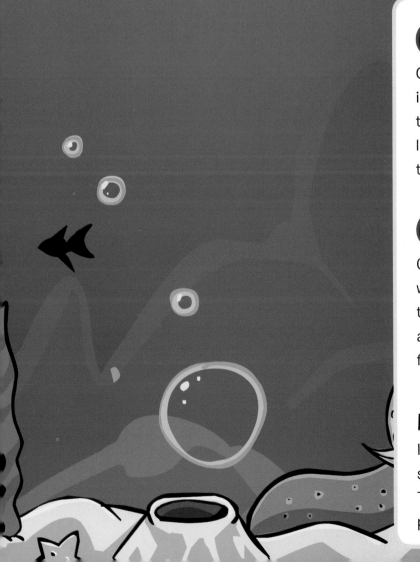

Playful Puffle

Click the *play* icon when pink puffles are in a playful mood and they'll do tricks with their jump ropes, like turning them into lassos. Click it again and they'll jump on their toy trampolines.

Hungry, Hungry Puffle

Give a pink puffle some bubble gum and it will blow the bubble up like a balloon until the puffle is floating in the air! If you give a pink puffle a cookie, it will run back and forth over the cookie before eating it.

More Puffle Stuff

In the bath, a pink puffle will put on a snorkel mask and disappear underwater. They rock from side to side when their penguin owners dance.

BLACK PUFFLE

Black puffles like to keep to themselves. They are quiet but they have a lot of personality. Black puffles are sometimes very energetic and they can be a bit mischievous. Even when they're well fed and taken care of, they still look a bit grumpy.

⚫ Playful Puffle

Click the *play* icon and a black puffle will ride its skateboard. It will do tricks and skate back and forth. Click it again and it'll turn red, light on fire, and fly around.

🍪 Hungry, Hungry Puffle

When a black puffle chews gum, it blows a giant bubble that explodes, covering itself in goo. Then it shakes the gum off. When it eats a cookie, it spins like a tornado, swirling back and forth on top of the cookie.

More Puffle Stuff

When a black puffle bathes, it turns red and bursts into flames! It gets so hot, the bathwater boils and evaporates, turning into a cloud. Then the cloud rains on the puffle. When a black puffle's penguin dances, the puffle spins like a tornado.

PURPLE PUFFLE

Purple puffles are very happy and they love to dance. But they are also pretty picky—especially when it comes to food.

🔵 Playful Puffle

If you click the *play* icon, a purple puffle will blow a bubble around itself and float in the air. Click the icon again and it will dance under a disco ball and even ride around on it.

🔵 Hungry, Hungry Puffle

A purple puffle can blow a bubble gum bubble within a bubble! If you give it a cookie, it won't eat it until whipped cream and a cherry magically appear on top. It won't eat its Puffle-Os until a saltshaker sprinkles salt on top.

More Puffle Stuff

After a purple puffle takes a bath, it spins its hair into several different hairstyles. When it dances, it moves from side to side, doing flips and even a tornado spin! And a purple puffle always wears its sleep mask when it snoozes.

YELLOW PUFFLE

Yellow puffles are the newest puffles on Club Penguin. They are known for being artistic, creative dreamers.

Playful Puffle

Click the *play* icon and a yellow puffle will put on a beret, and paint on its easel. Click it again and it will get out a director's chair and a movie camera, pretending to film a scene.

Hungry, Hungry Puffle

A yellow puffle likes to blow a bubble gum bubble and draw a face on it. If you give it a cookie, it will bite it into the shape of a mask and wear it before gulping it down. It will also turn its Puffle-Os into a sculpture and then eat it.

More Puffle Stuff

Yellow puffles take baths in tubs filled with paint! When they get out, they are covered in different paint colors—until they shake it all off. When its penguin dances, a yellow puffle sings. While sleeping, yellow puffles dream of being superheroes.

When you play the arcade game *Thin Ice* in the Dance Lounge, you get to be a black puffle on fire, trying to melt all the ice and get the pink jewel at the end of each level.

You and your red puffle can hang ten in *Catchin' Waves*. All you have to do is take your red puffle for a walk and enter *Catchin' Waves* together. It will surf right behind you and even help you score points.

AQUA GRABBER

Bring your pink puffle along when you play *Aqua Grabber*. It will appear next to you wearing scuba gear and will help you rescue treasure from the ocean floor.

ICE FISHING

Goin' fishin'? When you play *Ice Fishing* at the Ski Lodge, a pink puffle will swim across the screen in a scuba mask, giving you helpful hints.

PUFFLE ROUND-UP!

Help the Pet Shop catch wild puffles by playing *Puffle Round-Up*. It's easy! Just use your mouse to herd as many puffles as you can into the pen. Once you catch them, the Pet Shop will put them up for adoption. After all, each puffle deserves a happy home.